PEANUTS

Go to School, Charlie Brown!

Based on the comic strip and
characters created by Charles M. Schulz
Adapted by Judy Katchske
Art adapted by Tom Brannon

LITTLE SIMON
New York   London   Toronto   Sydney

LITTLE SIMON
An imprint of Simon & Schuster Children's Publishing Division
1230 Avenue of the Americas, New York, New York 10020
© 2004 by United Feature Syndicate, Inc. All rights reserved.
PEANUTS is a registered trademark of United Feature Syndicate, Inc.
All rights reserved, including the right of reproduction in whole or in part in any form.
LITTLE SIMON and colophon are registered trademarks of Simon & Schuster.
Manufactured in the United States of America
First Edition 10 9 8 7 6 5 4 3 2 1
ISBN 0-689-86818-9
Based on the comic strips by Charles M. Schulz

When Sally was younger she couldn't wait to go to school.
"I wish we could go to school, Snoopy!" she said. "But they won't let you go until you're five years old!"

And can prove that you're a human being, Snoopy thought.
But when the actual moment came, Sally changed her mind.

"Well, Sally," Charlie Brown told his sister. "In a couple of weeks you'll be starting kindergarten!"

Sally's eyes popped wide open. "Kindergarten?" she gasped.

"Sure," Charlie Brown said. "Everybody has to go to school."

"School?" Sally cried.

When Sally thought of school she imagined the worst. Would she be a finger-painting flop? A show-and-tell shame? A recess reject?

"Isn't there any way I can get out of starting kindergarten?" Sally asked Linus.

"I doubt it, Sally," Linus answered. "Everybody has to go to school."

"I'm not the going-to-school type," Sally protested. "I can't remember where the longest river is. Or how high all those mountains are. I can't remember all those English kings!"

"I DON'T WANT TO GO TO KINDERGARTEN!" she wailed.

Sally dreaded the first day of kindergarten, so every day she asked Charlie Brown the same burning question: "Is today the first day of school?" "No," Charlie Brown replied. "One more week yet."

"Whew!" Sally said, sighing. "What a relief! I just wasn't ready. I don't know where my lunchbox is, and I don't know if my shoes are clean, and I haven't had my boiled egg yet!" Charlie Brown rolled his eyes.

"Next Tuesday should be quite a day," he said.

"I think your sister needs help, Charlie Brown," Linus said.
"Professional help!"

Charlie Brown thought about it. "Perhaps you're right," he agreed.

Charlie Brown sent Sally to see Lucy.
"My problem is that I'm afraid of kindergarten," Sally told Lucy.
"I don't know why. I think about it all the time. I'm really afraid."
"You're no different from anyone else," Lucy said. "Five cents, please."

"I want to talk to you, Charlie Brown," said Lucy. "As your sister's consulting psychiatrist, I must put the blame for her fears on you!"

"On me?" exclaimed Charlie Brown.

"I've gotta blame somebody," said Lucy. "It doesn't solve anything, but it makes me feel better."

Sally still worried about kindergarten . . . day and night!
"Hey, big brother," Sally whispered. "Wake up!"
Charlie Brown blinked open his eyes. It was the middle
of the night, and Sally was standing next to his bed!
"What's the matter?" he asked.

"I want to ask you about school," Sally said. "What if you don't know where to go? Or you forget your lunch or get lost in the hallway? What if you can't remember your locker combination?"

Charlie Brown couldn't believe it. He knew *he* was a worrywart, but Sally was taking the cake!

"Are you supposed to bring a loose-leaf binder?" Sally asked. "How wide? Two holes or three?"

"Look," Charlie Brown told Sally. "Just stop worrying. Everything will be all right."

Finally Sally calmed down. Then she went back to her room and back to sleep.

But now Charlie Brown was wide awake!
"What if *I* forget my locker combination?" he worried.
Rats! Sally's fear of school was contagious!

On the first day of school Charlie Brown got a wake-up call.
"School!" Sally yelled at the top of her lungs.
Charlie Brown flipped off the bed.

"Today's the first day of school!" Sally shouted as she ran through the house. "Memorize those conjunctions! Name those rivers! Don't forget your locker combination! What's the capital of Venezuela?"

Charlie Brown sighed. "I think the summers are getting shorter."

Charlie Brown walked Sally to school. It was the longest walk of his entire life!

"There it is," Charlie Brown said, pointing. "There's your school!"

Sally stared at the red brick building. On the outside it looked like any old grade school. But on the inside were teachers! And pop quizzes! And locker combinations waiting to be forgotten!

"Auugh!" Sally yelled.

Charlie Brown watched his sister run away. Getting Sally to go to school was like flying a kite! Or kicking a football! Or getting his team to win a baseball game! It was—IMPOSSIBLE!

But finally Charlie Brown convinced Sally to go to school. She survived her first day of kindergarten—and even liked it!

"We sang songs and we painted pictures," Sally told Linus. "And we listened to stories and we colored with crayons. . . ."

"We had a wonderful time!" Sally declared. "I think
every child should go to kindergarten."

Charlie Brown was happy. He still couldn't fly a kite. Or kick a football. Or win a baseball game. But he did get his little sister to go to school!

Now . . . if only he could get Snoopy to go *home*!